wild kittens

D0118281

This book is dedicated to all the organizations and individuals who work each day for the benefit of the wild nondomestic cats of the world. These include the Canadian Nature Federation, Defenders of Wildlife, National Audubon Society, The National Wildlife Federation, The Sierra Club, The Nature Conservancy, The Wilderness Society, The World Wildlife Fund, and all the less known, but equally valuable groups around the world from which most of us have yet to hear.

wild kittens

by peggy bauer, photographs by peggy and erwin bauer

CHRONICLE BOOKS

SAN FRANCISCO

Copyright © 1995 by Peggy Bauer.

All rights reserved. No part of this book may be reproduced without written permission from the Publisher.

Book and cover design by Nancy Zeches, San Francisco. Printed in Hong Kong.

Library of Congress Cataloging-in-Publication Data available. ISBN: 0-8118-1012-7

Distributed in Canada by Raincoast Books, 8680 Cambie Street, Vancouver, B.C. V6P 6M9. 10 9 8 7 6 5 4 3 2 1

Chronicle Books, 275 Fifth Street, San Francisco, CA 94103

Photographs: front cover, Lynx kitten; back cover, African lion; page 2, Margay kitten.

The maps in this book indicate approximate ranges for the various species.

contents

These cubs are quite young, still timid, and far from the confident and adventurous individuals they will become.

People often think of cats as being aloof and independent. In reality, even wild cats are profoundly affected by human activities. In fact, of the approximately three dozen cat species, nearly all are declining in numbers and one-third are considered threatened with extinction. This situation results primarily from the destruction of cat habitat by encroaching human populations.

Eight "big cats" continue to cling to existence. In Africa, the lion, leopard, and cheetah are supreme; in the New World, cougars and jaguars are the largest cats; and in Asia and India, tigers, snow leopards, and clouded leopards live precariously in their shrinking territories. Four big cats are known as "great cats": lions, tigers, jaguars, and leopards do not purr, they roar, and their young are called cubs, not kittens, which are the offspring of the smaller cats.

introduction

Cats are often compared to dogs in habits and physical characteristics. Generally, the cats are larger and stronger than wild dogs, in large part, many observers believe, because they hunt alone and hence require exceptional strength and power to bring down their prey. The dogs are obviously more social, and as a group, they often have amazing endurance. They may travel for miles in foraging for food and can often sustain chases of many miles in pursuit of prey.

Unlike dogs, which often live in large, interdependent packs that share the chores of hunting and raising the young, cats seldom congregate. The only family bond is between mother and young. The female is responsible for feeding and training the young, except, of course, in African lion prides, in which responsibilities are shared. The mother's range generally overlaps that of the father cat. The male is, however, seldom allowed to approach the young (male cats are among the primary dangers faced by kittens). His duty is to keep other males of the same species (which are an even greater danger than himself) away from the kittens.

Because the mother cat must hunt frequently to feed her kittens, she is often gone from the den, further endangering them. Small cats bring food to the den for the young, but this is difficult for great cats. They often prey on very large animals, and the young are then escorted to the site of the kill.

Cats are typically secretive, solitary, and often nocturnal creatures. Many live in areas that are wild and inaccessible. They are difficult to study and to know. Yet they are essential to the balance of many ecological systems on the planet, and they deserve to be protected, for they are part of our home here on earth.

The most numerous cat in the Americas, bobcats currently range throughout much of the United States and into Mexico, living in forests, deserts, swamps, and mountains. Using primarily sight, not scent, to hunt, they feed on many types of prey, from rabbits to wild turkeys. Although bobcats spend most of their time on the ground, they are excellent climbers, using trees as resting spots and refuge from intruders.

The male bobcat does not share its territory with other males, but his range overlaps those of several females. Breeding season is in the winter. Following an eight-week gestation period, the female finds a den in dense undergrowth or under a fallen tree. A litter of usually three kittens is born in the spring, and by autumn the kittens can hunt with their parents. Both parents supply food to the newborn kittens, but during most of the year bobcats are loners. Once the kittens mature and leave the den, they will often move into distant regions and repopulate previously depleted ranges.

The lynx and the bobcat both inhabit large areas of North America; however, they do not share territories. The bobcat appears to be expanding its range, pushing the lynx out of regions where their territories overlap. The lynx is found primarily in Canada, the bobcat south of that region. Some biologists believe that the bobcat is more aggressive than the lynx because bobcats must compete with coyotes and cougars for survival.

Despite being heavily trapped in the 1970s, bobcats have thrived, in part because they live in widely spaced and diverse areas. Their intelligence and resourcefulness protect them from the dangers encountered by other wild cats that cannot adapt to their changing environment.

bobcat

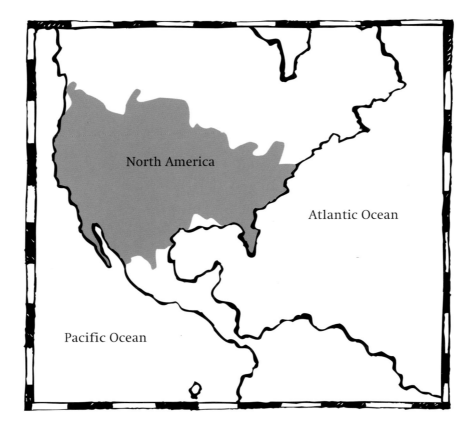

North America

Atlantic Ocean

Pacific Ocean

Because bobcats are so adaptable, they can settle in a great variety of habitats, finding a large number of suitable prey animals including birds such as yellow-bellied sapsuckers, pictured here, or American robins.

As the kittens grow, their natural curiosity and eagerness to roam become strong, and they begin to explore their home range.

The mother bobcat may return from hunting with a rabbit for her kittens or a mouse, as shown here. If there is not enough prey to sustain both her and her offspring, she will abandon them so that she herself may live to produce a litter the following year that has a better chance of survival.

At this early stage, the kittens lack mobility and strength, and their only response to any situation is vocal. They are surprisingly able to project their disquiet by mewing loudly in distress or purring contentedly when things are going well.

When three to five months of age, the young may accompany their mother for early hunting lessons. Of course at this early stage, they have no learned hunting skills at all, and may even have trouble making their way across the countryside. The kittens follow their mother, tumbling over deadfalls too wide to straddle, jumping, climbing trees and occasionally stopping to romp and stalk each other. Even when the undergrowth is rank and tall, the kittens can follow their mother by keeping an eye on her upturned tail and the ear patches that are easily visible.

These solitary cats, living in boreal forests and amid the snows of Canada and Alaska, are seldom seen. Because in the past it was heavily trapped, the lynx has disappeared from countries such as France and Italy where it was once plentiful. In Spain, the Iberian lynx is the most endangered carnivore in Europe.

Well adapted to their snowy world, lynx have exceptionally long legs, large, padded feet, and heavy coats. Because they are not swift runners, lynx are ambushers, crawling close to their prey or dropping on them from trees.

The life of the lynx is bound tightly and fatally with the snowshoe hare. When hare populations are high–they peak approximately every ten years–the lynx does well. In bad years, predator and prey both suffer. The hares feed on woody plants. Every few years, the plants, reacting to the assault of constantly increasing numbers of hares, produce a bitter chemical compound that hares cannot tolerate. The hares starve in great numbers, causing the lynx population to plummet. As the plants recover, the hare and lynx populations gradually increase again. A recent study found that when hares are abundant, 99 percent of lynx females reproduce; with small hare populations, only 10 percent of lynx females reproduce.

Female lynx usually have litters of two to four kittens, giving birth in a den prepared in a rock crevice or timber deadfall. A lynx family stays together until the mother is ready to mate again. Although fully grown at about thirty months, the young lynx still have a very high mortality rate, for theirs is a harsh environment where food is not always plentiful.

In North America, the lynx–as well as the bobcat and cougar–is doing well. Despite trapping depredations in the 1970s, its numbers appear to have increased, although accurate counts are difficult because of the cat's remote habitat and solitary habits.

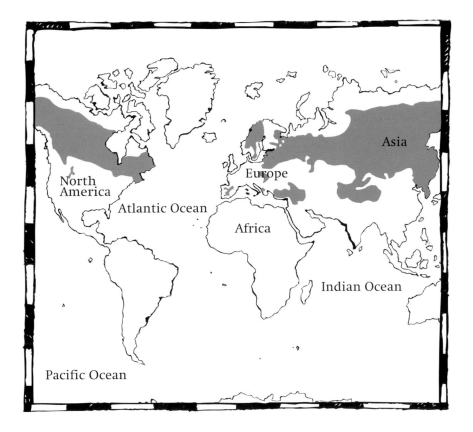

North America

Europe

Asia

North
America

Atlantic Ocean

Africa

Indian Ocean

Pacific Ocean

The kittens' eyes open at about two and a half weeks of age and by six weeks they can see well enough to explore the area near home. Although they nurse for five months, the youngsters begin eating meat early, from the thirteenth day onward.

Young males seem especially adventurous, although either sex can find itself in uncomfortable situations. This fearless lynx kitten walks on a branch and then loses its grip, hanging precariously. In the end it recovered itself and continued on.

The true habitat of the lynx is a boreal forest. The cats require a varied landscape with thick trees for denning and shelter and lakes and burned areas for hunting. A problem for lynx is logging, which clears great swaths of forest. The replacement trees that are grown as row crops alter the natural diversity of the landscape.

Lynx kittens, like other kittens and pups, huddle together for a feeling of security and warmth.

The hunting mother lynx will launch herself on great long legs from her hiding place in the brush to capture grouse (as pictured here), ground squirrels, mice, or rabbits.

Playing with prey by tossing it up and catching it, batting it with a big paw, and playing "crouch and pounce" sharpens the kittens' coordination and strengthens young muscles. This ruffed grouse was brought to the den by the mother.

Kittens follow their mother but seem to learn about the world more by trial and error than by example.

Young lynx enjoy new sights and sounds and explore near water where aquatic creatures such as frogs might be seen jumping or dragonflies alighting. Anything new is fascinating, and as they mature, the kittens gradually increase the distance they travel from the den entrance.

The cat that westerners call a cougar is known by other names as well: it is a panther in Florida, a puma, a painter, catamount, or a mountain lion elsewhere in the United States. It ranges from western Canada, through the United States, into Mexico and Central America, and all the way to the tip of South America. The cougar's territory was once even more extensive, but by the beginning of the twentieth century, the cats survived primarily in the rugged western mountains, with a few stragglers in Florida. By the 1980s, their numbers were relatively stable with twenty-three states hosting cougars.

Cougar populations have risen because of an increase in the size of forests and the number of deer in the eastern United States. Many observers believe cougars will continue to move into the eastern states as the habitats become better suited to the cats' needs. They have been reported in the Great Smoky Mountains National Park and in the Blue Ridge Parkway.

Cougars breed and produce young at any time of the year. However, the kittens are born primarily in the winter, when deer, the cougar's main prey, are hampered by deep snow and cannot easily flee. Generally, three to six offspring are in each litter. Males never assist with raising the cubs.

Cougars stalk their prey and strike from ambush. They also exhibit great adaptability in choosing prey. When deer are scarce, cougars feed on small mammals, reptiles, and rodents.

In several ways, cougars are unlike other cats: the kittens are spotted and their mother is unpatterned; the cougar's pupils are round, while most other cats have vertical slits; and this very large animal (second only to the jaguar in size) purrs like a domestic cat or chirps, sounding much like a bird.

cougar

North America

Atlantic Ocean

South America

Pacific Ocean

Kittens that are born in the spring accompany their mother on hunting trips by fall. With their growing strength and curiosity, these venture from the den site to explore, the first step toward self-sufficiency.

This cougar mother has selected a large, secure rock cave as a birthing area. Like many other cats, the cougar gives birth after a gestation period of about three months, but unlike other cats, the coat of the young does not match that of the parent. Cougar kittens are strongly marked with spots, contrasting with the mother's unpatterned pelage. At birth the tiny offspring weigh only about twelve ounces and measure about ten inches long.

The young eagerly nurse for three months, but if given the opportunity the kittens will continue until half grown. Even at six weeks, they eat meat. At six months the spots begin to disappear, and after several more months, the cats become, as their Latin name implies, "cats of one color," *Felis concolor*.

Another prey species is rabbit or hare, which is often easier to see when not hidden by the dense foliage of summer. Driven by hunger and instinct even a young cougar can be a successful hunter.

While her kittens are still quite small, the mother cougar leaves them in the den when she hunts.

The leopard is found over a wider area than any other big cat, in part because this highly adaptive animal feeds on a variety of prey. Of the three big cats of East Africa–lions, leopards, and cheetahs–the leopard falls between the others in strength. But while this cunning cat may not be as strong as a lion, its chances for survival are better. The larger cats are usually forced from an area by human intrusion, but leopards–which are as adaptable as cougars–are often able to change their habits to meet new conditions. Leopards can live in deserts, rain forests, or mountains.

Expert at using cover, leopards hunt by day or night, using their camouflage to blend with the surroundings. They are agile, but not particularly fast, so leopards hunt from ambush, leaping upon the backs of their prey. They also consume birds, rodents, fish, and reptiles such as pythons. Where they compete for prey with lions, the leopard stores its food in trees so lions, hyenas, and wild dogs cannot reach it.

Leopards have no particular breeding season. A litter is usually two to three cubs, which are not really capable hunters until they reach two years.

Although often considered endangered, leopards exist in substantial numbers. Some observers put their number in Africa at 900,000. Unfortunately, in other parts of the globe, from Asia to the Pacific, their survival is threatened.

leopard

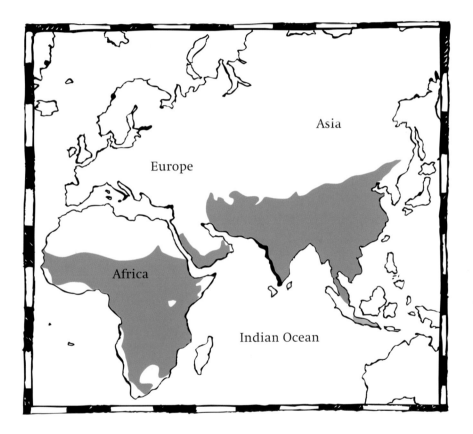

Europe

Asia

Africa

Indian Ocean

Leopard cubs are nearly always left by the mother in a rock crevice or in dense brush, but occasionally one is left (or moves itself) into a tree. Even a tree covered with thorns seems to pose no problem.

The bond between mother leopards and their young is strong, and may be particularly so when there is only a single cub. All attention and care are lavished on the single cub. Then too, leopard cubs are left alone for extended periods, so the return of the mother is an especially joyous occasion.

Cubs nap often, and shallow ditches like this one make perfect beds.

Early in the cub's life, when it is still quite small, it sleeps much of the time when the mother is absent. But as it grows older, it amuses itself by playing with any handy bit of brush, by climbing a small tree, or by practicing an effective stalk. These activities promote strength and coordination. Tree climbing will become a valuable skill in later life, when the leopard spends much time in trees and will have the ability to scale a vertical trunk carrying a large prey animal. The meal will be wedged securely above ground, safe from the attentions of other carnivores.

When the leopard cubs are small, they do not yet eat meat. But one day the cub licks its mother's bloody muzzle and acquires a taste for meat.

When a female leopard returns to her cubs with a kill, the cub will imitate its mother by grabbing the prey by the neck and dragging it to the brush as she would.

The King of Beasts ranges over eastern and southern Africa, living in groups called prides, which are based around related females and their young. Each pride averages fifteen animals, with few males, since the male cubs are driven from the pride when they reach maturity at two years. Lions are the only big cats with a cooperative organization that involves caring for the young and hunting.

During the day, the pride usually relaxes, sometimes in trees, but usually on the ground. Toward evening they begin to stir, preparing for the night's hunt. The females of the pride are adept stalkers and do most of the hunting, primarily from ambush. When hunting, the female lions may be away from the den for one or two days. At this time, active defense of the den and the cubs is vital to prevent attacks by leopards, hyenas, and wild dogs. Because the male's larger size makes it more powerful, it is often the defender of the pride's territory and young. Nonetheless, a solitary male lion, even without the pride's numbers to assist him, is still a formidable and successful hunter.

Lions depend more upon sight and sound than scent in hunting. They are opportunistic, feeding upon anything that is easy to catch. Birds, rodents, and other small animals are occasionally caught, but the primary food is large mammals. They will also steal prey from other animals.

Although the survival rate of lion cubs is poor, the East African population seems stable at several thousand. The incursion of humans and the demands for more agricultural land are the greatest threats to lions, which depend upon the vast herds of the savanna for survival.

african li

Africa

Atlantic Ocean

Indian Ocean

African lions, more than any other wild cat, show affection for each other. Sisters rub foreheads, lion and lioness slide the entire length of their bodies together, but most attention is lavished on the cubs, which seldom stray from their mother's side.

The flicking tail of an adult is always a fascinating target to pounce upon, and often cubs play and fight until they tire of the game.

Lionesses typically hunt at dusk. A single lioness returns to the pride with her catch, a young impala fawn.

These tiny cubs came from two mothers who had left the pride to give birth deep in the bush. Frightened at first, the young gradually moved, as a group, none willing to leave the safety inherent in numbers.

As a rule, all cubs of a pride have nearly the same birthdays. Young males like this one are typically more aggressive than their sisters and will snarl at the slightest provocation.

A female drags the meager remains of a zebra beneath a shrub, while the cubs do their best to eat the moving meal.

Abroad day or night, the tiger encounters few natural enemies as it roams its vast range. The tiger generally feeds on large herbivores of the forest, but it will also consume crocodiles, turtles, and even young elephants. After a kill, the tiger may drag its victim to a secluded spot before eating.

These big cats are usually solitary, but since their territories are so large, male tigers may occasionally interact with other males in hunting, cooperating to bring down the prey and to share in the spoils. The hunting territory of a male usually overlaps that of several females, facilitating mating. Although the male may remain with the female for a few days after mating, it does not help to raise the young.

The cats are quite prolific, giving birth to six or seven cubs after a three-month gestation period. The cubs and the mother are the principal social group, the male being absent. In fact, predatory male tigers have been identified as one of the major causes of cub mortality, and the female goes to great lengths to keep males away from the young. The family group typically separates when the cubs are two years old, although Siberian tiger cubs may remain with their mother until they are three or four.

Tigers once ranged over most of Asia, but human encroachments have severely limited their range and survival. Although tigers can withstand great extremes of temperature, most of the big cats now live in relatively warm forested areas. Unfortunately, their existence is threatened by increasing human populations and by poachers who sell the animals' parts for use in traditional Asian medicines. Its reputation as a killer of humans has also led to its being heavily hunted in areas of increasingly dense human populations.

tiger

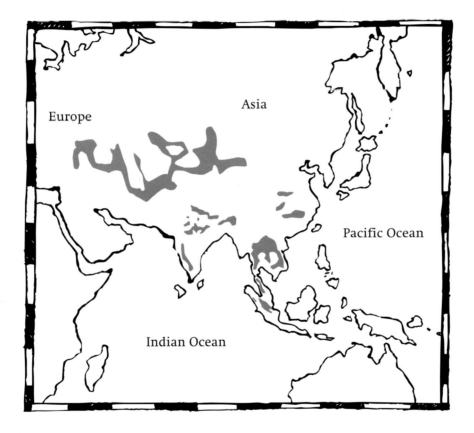

Europe

Asia

Pacific Ocean

Indian Ocean

Whether to prompt a sibling into a wrestling game or to signify subordination or just to feel the ground on its back, tiger cubs often tumble and wiggle with their paws in the air.

Getting to know the world often means using the mouth to test the surroundings. A tiger cub tentatively bites limber little twig that almost, but not quite, fights back.

The white ear patches are common to many members of the cat family. Some observers believe they allow young cats to easily follow an adult.

Although young tigers are born with very functional claws and an inquisitive personality, their legs, which will be long and strong in the adult cat, are still short and stumpy in the cub, and eyes that will spot a monkey high in the tree canopy are, at this stage, barely able to coordinate.

Twigs in the way present no problem to a determined cub.

Bengal (Indian) tigers are very fond of water and often laze beside a forest pool or actually soak in the water when the temperatures soar. Tigers do not seem well adapted to hot weather and appear to suffer in the heat.

Cheetahs are known for their quickness (they are the fastest of all land mammals). Chasing, not stalking or ambush, is their preferred method of attack. Unlike other big cats, cheetahs are designed more for speed than power, having long legs, a small head, and claws that work better at maintaining traction than hooking prey. They live in open grasslands where they can utilize their agility to hunt.

Small antelope are the cheetah's favored prey. It hunts during the day, moving as close as possible to its victim before bursting from cover in a blinding rush of speed, which the cat can only sustain for about 500 yards. Following a successful kill, the cheetah eats immediately, because it does not have the strength to protect the food from threats by hyenas or lions. Cheetah brothers may band together to hunt, a practice not common to most other big cats. Cheetah families separate before the kittens are two years old, but brothers and sisters may stay together for much longer.

But even its speed has not kept the cheetah from being threatened with extinction. These big cats suffer from a genetic weakness that threatens their survival. Approximately 10,000 years ago, during one of the earth's periodic ice ages, all but a small group of cheetahs died. The survivors repopulated their area, but inbreeding left males with genetic abnormalities leading to low conception rates. In addition, these timid cats do not adapt well to changing conditions.

Cheetahs may have as many as eight kittens in their litters, but they also have a high mortality rate. The solitary cheetah mother must make a kill every day when she has kittens. During this time, the kittens are left alone, so the vulnerable cheetahs have evolved an interesting method for avoiding marauding lions, leopards, and hyenas. Cheetah kittens closely resemble the ratel–also known as the honey badger–a powerful and aggressive creature of the savanna that most other animals avoid if possible, so predators are inclined to keep their distance from the small cheetahs.

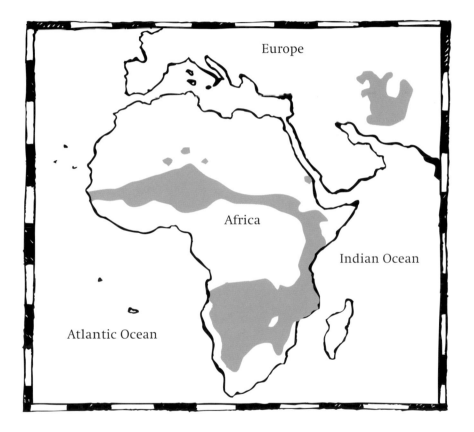

Europe

Africa

Indian Ocean

Atlantic Ocean

63

Small antelope, such as this Thompson's gazelle, are a basic food source for cheetahs.

The cheetah is the swiftest of Africa's three large cats, its speed reaching 70 miles per hour over a short distance. The cheetah cannot sustain this velocity for long, however, and its hunting successes must come quickly or not at all.

Of the three large cats in Africa—the lion, leopard, and cheetah—the cheetah is the most lightly built, has the smallest teeth for body size, and lacks retractable claws. When there is a showdown, such as over possession of a kill, leopards will give way to lions, and cheetahs will retreat from both.

Cheetah kittens enjoy playing with each other and will even share meals without squabbling. After eating, they often lick each other's muzzles clean.

The ocelot is one of the few spotted cats to be seen in the United States, occasionally being found in southwest Texas or Arizona. Before large sections of the Rio Grande Valley were cleared, they inhabited that region plus the coastal areas of Central America, Mexico, and parts of South America.

Today, the ocelot is found mainly in Central and South America where they may live in areas ranging from semi-desert to rain forests. Ocelot kittens are thought to make better household pets than the young of other wild cats; however, this early docility evaporates when the kitten reaches maturity.

Although the ocelot is a good climber, it hunts primarily on the ground, capturing small prey, such as snakes, birds, and reptiles.

Unhappily, ocelots have long been threatened throughout most of their range. They have a luxurious pelt, so they have been extensively trapped. Recent studies indicate that laws protecting the ocelot have succeeded, and their numbers are beginning to increase gradually.

ocelot

South America

Pacific Ocean

Atlantic Ocean

As the kittens grow, they explore more widely around the den area, sometimes climbing trees, although they are not truly arboreal, preferring to run down prey on the ground.

The coats of the spotted cats like the ocelot are well suited to their habitat, providing good camouflage in most situations.

This young ocelot is happy to remain in a tree as long as the bird above holds its attention.

Like many cats, ocelots play with their prey. Here, an unfortunate iguana is the ocelot's toy as well as a meal.

other kittens and cubs

The margay kittens stay close to the mother
during the nursing period, which lasts two
months.

Little is known about the life of the clouded leopard. They do not seem to mind the water, although they do not swim willingly. This cat watches fish in a quiet pool, only moving when the fish come near the edge.

Many small cats live almost unknown in various parts of the world. They are usually few in number, and because they inhabit remote and often inhospitable regions, they are not frequently studied.

African wild cat Regarded as the ancestor of the domestic cat, this wild cat lives in parts of Africa and Asia.

Black-footed cat At four pounds, this smallest of all wild cats lives in the southern dry belt of Africa. It is nocturnal and often hides in abandoned termite mounds

Caracal Its name is derived from Turkish and means "black ears." The caracal – or desert lynx – lives in open habitats and semi-arid regions throughout India, Asia Minor, and most of Africa, where it hunts birds and rodents.

Clouded Leopard Of all wild cats, this may be the most beautifully patterned and the least known. Few remain in their Southeast Asia tropical forest range, which has been decimated in recent years. Population estimates are between only six thousand and seven thousand.

European wild cat Now found mainly in the Scottish highlands, this cat once ranged throughout Europe. Solitary and ferocious, it often attacks dogs or humans without apparent cause.

Geoffroy's cat This wild cat is heavily hunted for its fur. An excellent swimmer and climber, it lives primarily in the Andes.

Golden cat Also called Temminck's cat, this wild cat inhabits coastal forests in Africa and southeast Asia. Very little is known about these cats, except that they hunt by day or night and are adept at capturing birds and rodents.

Jaguar This largest of New World cats range in areas from Mexico through Central America and into South America. The gestation period is about three months, after